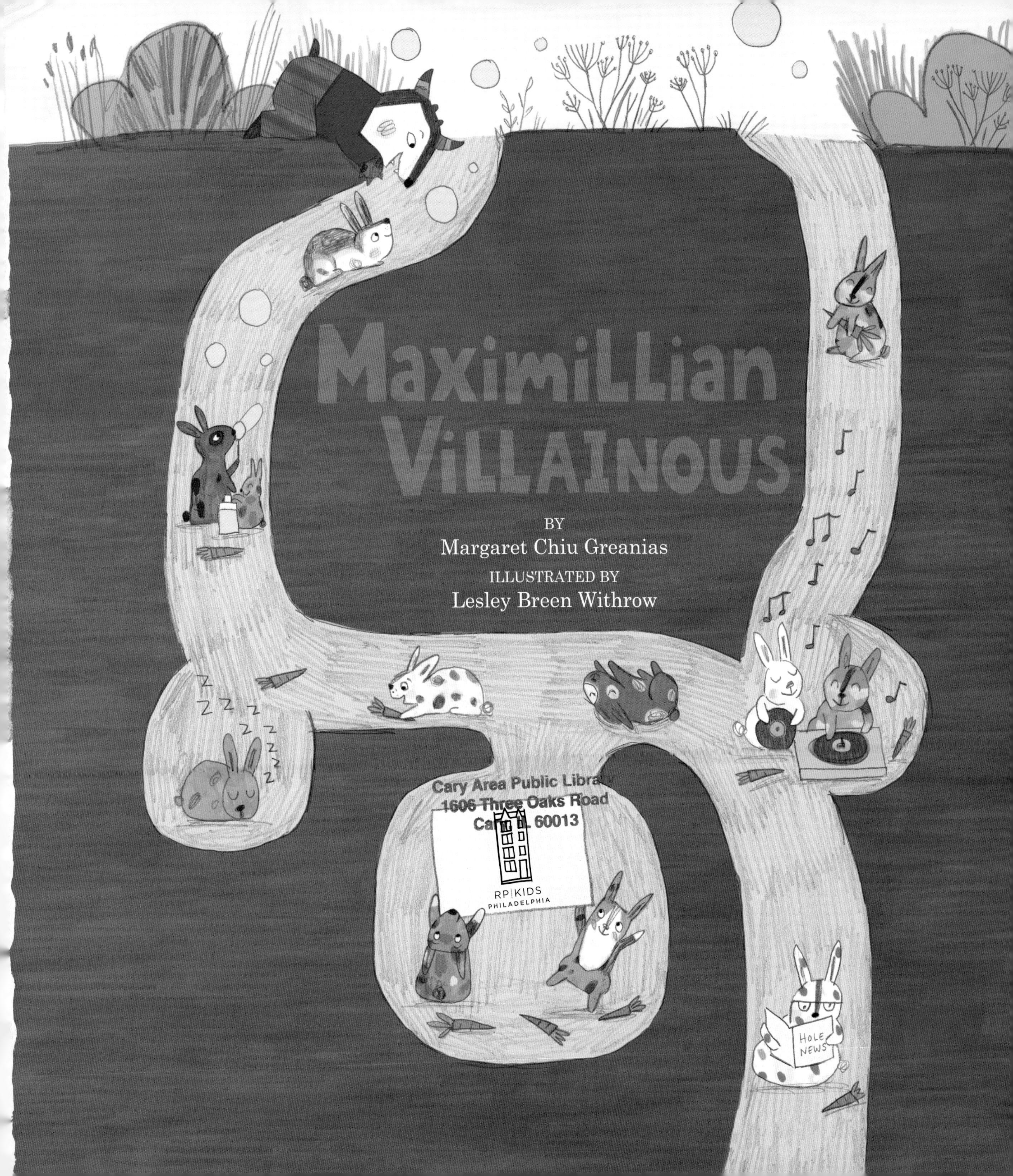

Maximillian Villainous

BY
Margaret Chiu Greanias
ILLUSTRATED BY
Lesley Breen Withrow

RP|KIDS
PHILADELPHIA

Running Press Kids
Hachette Book Group
1290 Avenue of the Americas, New York, NY 10104
www.runningpress.com/rpkids
@RP_Kids

Printed in China

First Edition: August 2018

Published by Running Press Kids, an imprint of Perseus Books, LLC, a subsidiary of Hachette Book Group, Inc.

The Hachette Speakers Bureau provides a wide range of authors for speaking events. To find out more, go to www.hachettespeakersbureau.com or call (866) 376-6591.

The publisher is not responsible for websites (or their content) that are not owned by the publisher.

Design by T. L. Bonaddio.

Library of Congress Control Number: 2016963267

ISBNs: 978-0-7624-6297-1 (hardcover), 978-0-7624-6298-8 (ebook), 978-0-7624-9174-2 (ebook), 978-0-7624-9175-9 (ebook)

1010

10 9 8 7 6 5 4 3 2 1

To Rob and my little minions:
Katie, Jack, and Alex.
May you always feel loved and accepted for who you are.
—M.C.G.

For my favorite little monsters:
Marin, Amanda, Leah, and Owen.
—L.B.W.

Maximillian Villainous came from
a long line of famous villains.
But Max was different from his family.

When his father stole
Santa's sleigh, Max gave Santa
keys to the family car.

When his grandfather
robbed the Tooth Fairy,
Max left her an apology
and his piggy bank.

When his mother
swiped Mother Nature's
powers, Max sent
Mother Nature to the spa.

The family groaned.
"*How* is Max
a Villainous?"

One day, Max brought home a bunny.

"I named him Bart," he said. "Can I keep him? Pretty please with spikes on top?"

His mother bristled. "Maximillian, my poison, we are Villainous. A bunny is *not* a suitable sidekick."

Max protested.

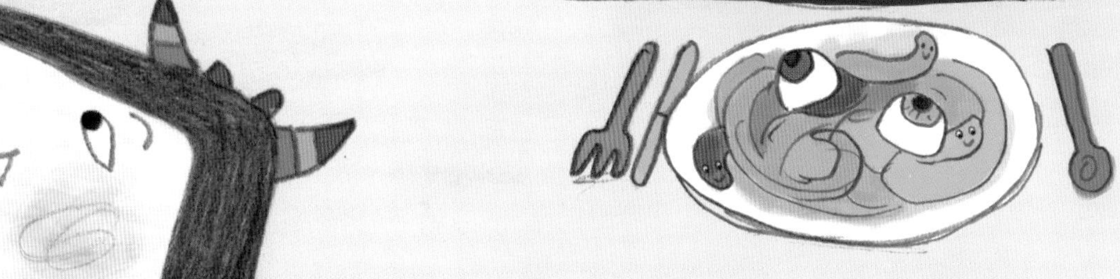

He pleaded.

He pestered.

"Please, oh please, oh p l e e e e e e e a s e?"

"Fine," his mother said. "But you must prove you are a devious duo. Succeed at *one* of these villainous tasks—and he's yours."

"Otherwise . . ." she said, "the bunny hops."

“Don’t worry, Bart.
I’ll think of something,”
said Max.
“We’ll steal . . . a pot of gold.”

Max built a
leprechaun trap.

But he hated to watch *anyone* walk into a trap.

"Oops."

"Max, Max, Max," said his father.
"Goodness grates on me!" said his grandfather.
"That bunny is utterly harebrained," said his mother.

Bart twitched.
"I'm *not* giving up," said Max.

Next, they snuck up on Cupid.

Should be easy to make a baby cry,
Max thought.

But it wasn't in their nature to pinch or poke.

They simply . . . patted.

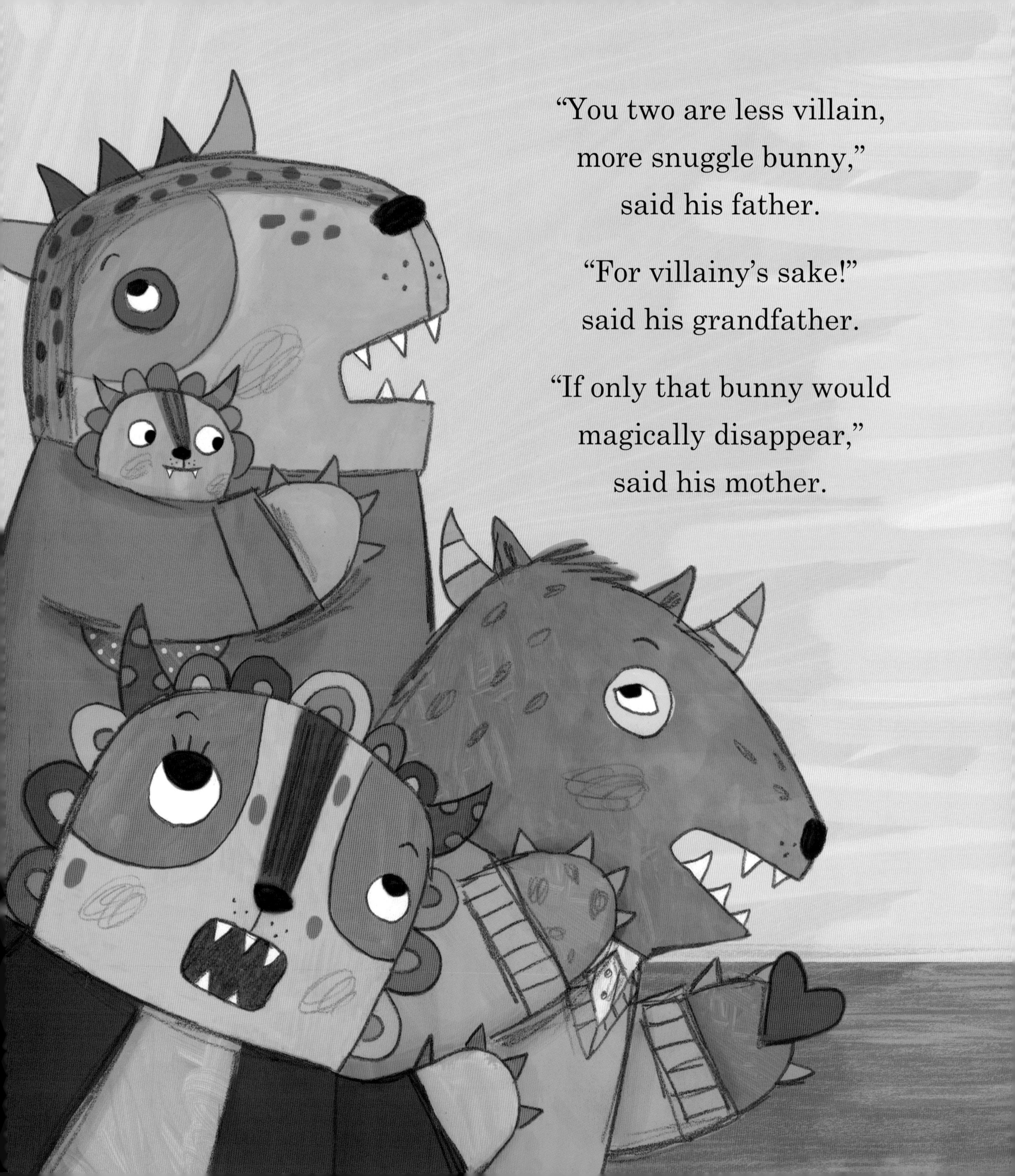

"You two are less villain,
more snuggle bunny,"
said his father.

"For villainy's sake!"
said his grandfather.

"If only that bunny would
magically disappear,"
said his mother.

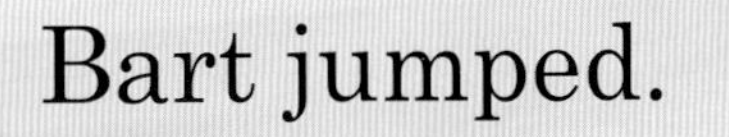

Bart jumped.

Max started to sweat.

They just *had* to succeed
in a spectacular way
and become famous.
No more Mr. Nice Max.

Max and Bart spread word
throughout the bunny underground.

“Love to dig? Join the bunny brigade!”

JOIN US!
JOIN US ABOVE
JOIN US!
HOLE NEWS

They planned to plunder the Sandman's stash of magic sleeping dust.

"Gentlebunnies!" Max yelled. "Commence the digging!"

Except . . .

Z Z Z Z Z Z Z Z Z

Z z z z z z z z . . .

It *couldn't* get any worse. But it did.
As they all were trudging home . . .

“Look! A bunny parade!” shouted a little girl.

Kids flocked to watch. Some even joined in.

"Oh, evil up already!" said his father.

"Thirteen generations of first-class villainy wiped out by a bunny," said his grandfather.

"If that bunny is still here tomorrow, I will launch him into space," said his mother.

Max felt sick. He couldn't imagine life without Bart. The little bunny had stolen his—

Suddenly, Max had it.

A positively devious idea!

"Mua-ha-HA!"

Max and Bart gathered their Bunny Brigade . . .

and matched bunnies,
one by one, with lonely
people everywhere.

They *stole* hearts,

made people *cry* (happy tears),

and *gained fame* for
their kind, thoughtful act.
Max and Bart *were*
a devious duo!
The family was
flabbergasted.

"Tricky," said his father.

"You've outfoxed us," said his grandfather.

"My ray of darkness, clearly you take after me," said his mother. "Bart, welcome to the family. I'm stealing these newspapers. I want to share them with all your aunts and uncles."

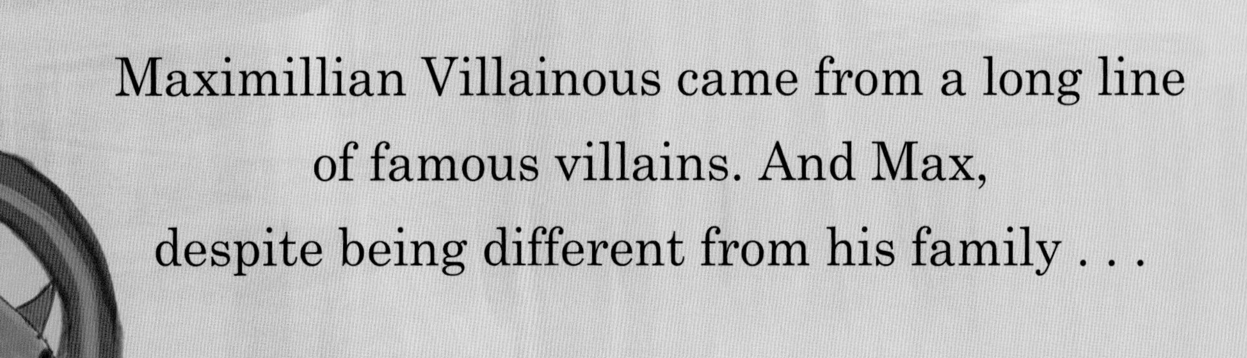

Maximillian Villainous came from a long line
of famous villains. And Max,
despite being different from his family . . .

. . . was a Villainous after all.